THE GOOSE GUARDS

TERRY DEARY'S ROMAN TALES

THE GOOSE GUARDS

Illustrated by Helen Flook

A & C Black • London

First published 2008 by
A & C Black Publishers Ltd
38 Soho Square, London, W1D 3HB

www.acblack.com

Text copyright © 2008 Terry Deary
Illustrations copyright © 2008 Helen Flook

ISBN 978-0-7136-8963-1

A CIP catalogue for this book is available from the British Library.

This book is produced using paper that is made from wood grown in
managed, sustainable forests. It is natural, renewable and recyclable.
The logging and manufacturing processes conform to the
environmental regulations of the country of origin.

Printed and bound in Great Britain by Cox & Wyman Ltd.

ONE

Rome, 387 BC

Rome is built on seven hills, they say. And the greatest hill is the Capitol Hill. And on that hill stand three mighty temples:

The temple of Jupiter – king of the gods.

The temple of Juno – queen of the gods.

And the temple of Minerva, the goddess of wisdom.

Three mighty gods, and their greatest duty was to guard the city of Rome.

And they did ... but only just! When I was a boy, I was a young priest at the temple of Juno. It was the most exciting time of my life, I can tell you, but the hardest time, too. We never stopped working.

In the mornings, we had lessons with the head priest, Marius. He liked shouting at me. No, he *loved* shouting at me.

"Brutus!" he sneered, as if I were a beetle that had crawled from inside his bread. "Brutus, tell me the name of the god of *weeding*?"

"Er... er..." I stammered.

The black-haired, brown-eyed girl next to me smirked seeing me suffer. Her name was Fabia and she was slippery sly.

"Insitor," she whispered from the corner of her mouth.

"Insitor!" I cried out. "Insitor ... the god of weeding, sir."

The face of Marius looked like a thundercloud. He spoke slowly, the way you speak to a baby. "Insitor is the god of *sowing seeds*. The god of weeding is ... who? Tell him, Fabia."

"Please, sir, the god of weeding is Sarritor," she smiled and showed her pointed, dog teeth.

"Well done, Fabia," Marius said and the thundercloud lifted. He almost smiled. "As for you, Brutus," he sighed. "What are we going to do with you?"

"Send him to weed the fields for a day," Fabia said quickly. "He can spend the whole day praying to Sarritor, and that will help him learn."

"Splendid idea, Fabia," the high priest said. "To the fields, Brutus," he ordered. "To the fields!"

TWO

I trudged down from the temple of
Juno, past the great, white geese that
grazed the grass. My mind was a
jumble of thoughts. I knew I had to
have revenge on Fabia, but I didn't
know how.

Then I saw the geese and I knew. Fabia had one great love. Those geese.

The geese were the holy birds of the goddess Juno. They even had their own junior priestess to feed and care for them. And who was that junior priestess? Yes, Fabia, of course.

So if the geese were harmed,
who would be upset? *Fabia*.

If a single goose was killed in the
night, who would be punished?
Fabia.

My feet felt as light as if I was
wearing the sandals of Mercury –
the ones with wings.

The geese. If I hurt the geese,
I would hurt Fabia. And that was
all I wanted in the world.

The ugly white monsters snaked
their long necks and hissed and
snapped at me. Oh, I would enjoy
having a chop at one of those necks!

But when I walked down the path
from the temple into Rome, I heard

the screams of the people. I saw the
terror in their faces as they ran from
their homes holding bundles of
their riches. Some items spilled out
in the dusty roadway, but they didn't
stop to pick them up.

A group of Roman soldiers ran after them; they were bleeding and sweating and throwing away their armour to help them run. One stopped at the great square to get his breath.

"What's happening?" I cried.

The man stood trembling and exhausted. His eyes were empty and haunted. I shook him hard and shouted again. "What happened?"

He began to babble. "We went to fight the Gaul armies in the hills to the north – they swept down and drove us back. They were so fierce – they fought with no armour – some had no clothes at all!

"And their battle cries. What a noise! More frightening than thunder. Most Romans turned and ran. They won't stop till they reach the rest of the Roman army in Veii. That's where I'm heading," he finished and staggered off down the street.

The roads were empty now.

Rome had run away.

I looked towards the north gate and saw why. The dust clouds showed that a mighty army was approaching.

THREE

The Gauls were coming. There would be no weeding for me in the fields that day – that dreadful day of 18th July.

I decided to run back up to the temples. I'd warn the priests and the guards. We'd block the only path to the Capitol Hill. We'd be safe.

I turned, and stopped. Some servants were carrying heavy ivory seats out of the senate – the great hall where the mighty men of Rome met up. They placed the huge

thrones in a line, facing the north
gate – facing the Gauls.

It was madness, I thought. A row
of seats wouldn't stop the barbarian
attackers. I wanted to run, but my
legs refused to move. I had to watch.

When the seats were in position, a dozen old men – the senators – walked out of the building. They were wearing fine togas with purple edges and each carried a rod – the rod that showed their power.

No one spoke. All we could hear in the warm morning air were the distant cries of the Gauls.

The old men sat on the thrones,
held their rods across their laps and
faced the gate.

"What are they doing?" I asked
a servant, as he backed away to the
safety of a dark alley.

"Waiting to die," he squeaked
and vanished.

There was a great roar and the first Gauls burst through the northern gateway and ran down the street. When they reached the square, they stopped. Many of them were naked, as the Roman soldier had said. Their pale bodies were streaked with sweat and blood and dust. Each carried a sword and a shield.

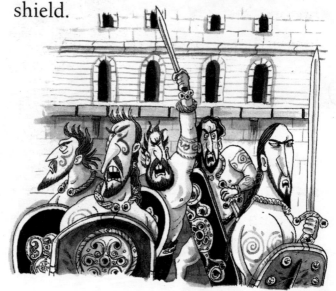

The Gauls formed a line, facing the senators. The old Romans didn't move. A breeze stirred their white beards, or they could have been statues.

The Gauls looked around. They seemed to fear a trap. At last a massive warrior in fine armour pushed his way forward and faced the senators. He shouted at them in some strange tongue. No one moved. Then he spoke in rough Latin, and I understood.

"I am Brennus, king of the Gauls.
Rome is now in my power and you
must kneel at my feet."

The senators stared straight ahead
and ignored him.

Brennus turned red in the face.
"Bow, you beaten old fools," he
screamed, then he marched up
to one of the senators, old Papirius,

and shouted in his face. "What is it
you Romans say? *Vae victis*, isn't it?
Woe to the defeated!"

Papirius did not move.

One of Brennus's captains stepped
forward. "You insult our king – that
insults us all!" He reached forward,
grasped the old man's beard and
pulled it.

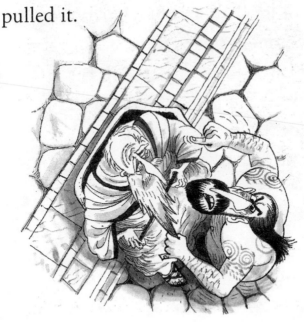

What happened next was so quick, I could hardly take it in. Papirius raised his rod of power and smashed it on to the hand that tugged his beard. The captain gave a roar, raised his sword and brought it down on Papirius's head. The old man fell, dead. Then the other Gauls leapt forward and butchered the senators in their seats.

I ran. At last my legs felt the winged sandals of Mercury again. I flew up the Capitol Hill.

"*Vae victis!*" I cried. "*Vae victis ...* woe to the defeated!"

FOUR

Three weeks passed after I fled
from the dead senators. They were
frightening times.

There was only one path to the Capitol Hill, so it was easy for our temple troops to defend it. The Gauls who rushed up the hill were chopped down, just as they had slaughtered the senators.

The Gauls who fled back down the hill started burning and robbing the city below us in revenge.

The temples stood on the edge of a cliff and no army could climb the cliff. Far below were sharp rocks – one day a priestess had been thrown on to the rocks to die – the priestess Tarpeia – so they were known as the Tarpeian Rocks.

As the sun set over the sea, I gazed down on the smoking ruins of the city and the Gauls camped in the streets. When I looked at those rocks, I dreamed that one day the foul Fabia would have a little accident and end up there.

Fabia slid alongside me. "What are you thinking, Brutus?" she asked.

"I was thinking about Tarpeia ...
and worried you might end up like
her. You will be careful, won't you?"

"I will," she said quietly.

She believed that I was worried
about her!

"Of course," she went on, "Tarpeia
was crushed to death between the
enemy shields before they threw her
off this cliff ... she wouldn't have felt
a thing."

Crushed to death first? No, I
wouldn't mind if that happened to
Fabia, I decided.

"What will happen, Brutus?" she asked.

The cruel, sly girl was as tired and starving as the rest of us. Her spirit seemed as crushed as Tarpeia's body.

"We'll survive. Lord Furius has the army at Veii – he'll rescue us," I said.

The sun slid out of sight and shadows raced over the land. That's when I saw a movement at the foot of the cliff. Someone was climbing the steep, secret path that only the Romans knew about.

"Hush!" I whispered to Fabia and ran to find the captain of the guard, Marcus Manlius. He was at the gates to the path – waiting for another attack there. No one thought the Gauls would try to climb the cliffs.

Marcus Manlius was a powerful man with the eyes of a hawk and a nose like its beak. He listened to my babbled news, then he took off his hob-nailed sandals so he could run silently to the cliff edge.

Pulling Fabia back, Marcus stared down into the gloom. "Someone is climbing the cliff," he nodded. "Well done, boy."

He backed away and we hid behind one of the great marble columns of the temple. When we heard a young man pulling himself over the top of the Tarpeian cliff, Marcus Manlius leapt out.

"Die, Gaul!" he cried.

FIVE

As Fabia and I ran out to watch, we saw the shadowy form of the invader fall to his knees, throw his arms wide and cry, "I am not armed – I am a friend – I am a Roman!"

He spoke Latin and wore a Roman tunic. Marcus lowered his sword and helped him to his feet.

"I've come to help," the man panted. "I am Cominius."

Fabia snorted. "One man can't do much!"

The stranger peered at her through the darkness. "One man with an army behind him can," he said.

"Oh," Fabia muttered, and I felt pleased to see her squashed.

"Lord Furius has the army ready to attack," Cominius explained.

"But he needs orders. He needs me to return and tell him you wish to be rescued."

Marcus Manlius led the way to
the temple where the priests and the
soldiers were eating a miserable
meal of corn and watery wine. "My
friends, we have news from Lord
Furius," he said. "The army is
gathered at Veii. He wants to know
if we want his help."

Marius rose to his feet. Like Fabia, his manner was quiet and tired now. "Lord Furius was banished from Rome. He is a rogue and we sent him away for his crimes."

Marcus Manlius said, "Then we can stay here and die. The Gauls will overrun the temples. They will pull down the statues of our gods.

The past three weeks of struggle will have been wasted. We may as well have given in on that first day. Is that what you want, Marius?"

Marius shook his head wearily. "Let us send for Furius," he conceded.

The young soldier, Cominius, thanked him and set off back down the secret path to Veii.

Everyone on the Capitol Hill was cheered by the thought of rescue.

"It will take two days for Furius to reach us. We have barely enough food to live on." He laughed. "It would be good to have a feast when they arrive. But we can't."

And that's when I stepped forward. It was the plan I'd been dreaming of for days.

"There *is* a way we can eat like lords," I said brightly.

"How?" Marcus asked.

I turned and looked at Fabia. "By killing those great, fat geese, of course!" I said.

"No!" she screamed. "Not the geese! You can't! They're holy birds and we need them to protect Rome!" She wailed and sobbed till she was too tired to cry any longer.

But Marcus Manlius nodded. "When rescue comes, we will feast on the geese," he agreed.

I smiled to myself. My revenge was almost complete.

SIX

I walked past the geese the next
morning. They clacked their yellow
beaks at me and hissed
their hatred.

But that day I smiled and licked my lips. "Tomorrow, my feathered friends. Tomorrow, we'll be rescued by Lord Furius and then I will eat you. That'll be nice ... for me ... won't it?"

I walked off, laughing, and on my way I passed the tearful Fabia going to give the geese their last-ever meal.

The head priest Marius didn't shout at me in class that day. He taught us the right way to sacrifice a goat.

"It is wrong to kill an animal if it doesn't want to be killed," he told us. "What you must do is hold out some food. The animal will stretch out its neck to take it. That is a sign that it wants to have its throat cut. Then you cut it."

Fabia was silent.

"Will it work with the geese, sir?" I asked eagerly, and I heard Fabia let out a small sob.

"Probably," Marius sighed. "But I am not sure that we should be sacrificing the holy geese..."

"Of *course* we shouldn't," Fabia sniffled. "They're Rome's protectors."

"But they didn't save Rome, did they?" I jeered. I turned back to Marius. "Can I be there when you kill them?"

The priest nodded. "Unless we receive a sign from the gods," he said, and I sighed with happiness.

You must be thinking I was cruel and spiteful. You are right. I wanted to hurt Fabia, so I wasn't thinking about the geese. Boys can be stupid and blind.

Marius said the geese needed a miracle if they were going to live. And I suppose what happened that night was a miracle...

While I had been tormenting the geese, and Fabia, that morning, the Gaul guards at the foot of the cliffs had seen the broken branches and crushed plants on the cliff. It was the trail Cominius had left when he climbed down to get help. Now the Gauls knew there was a way up.

King Brennus had seen us beat his men on the path to the Capitol Hill. He knew that the Gauls had no chance of succeeding by climbing a narrow, slippery cliff path.

"We must go in the dark," the king decided. "There is no moon tonight," he told his captains. "Twenty of the best warriors can climb the cliff, kill the guards and take the Capitol Hill. If we hold that hill, when the Roman army attacks, they will never drive us out!"

SEVEN

And so they set about their plan.

In the temples, we ate our thin corn porridge and settled down to sleep. It would be our last night of misery. Tomorrow Furius would come with the Roman army. Tomorrow we would feast on goose flesh.

I slept. The priests slept. Our leader Marcus Manlius slept. The guards and even the guard dogs slept.

Everyone was exhausted.

Through the night, the Gauls climbed. In the darkest hour they reached the top of the cliff. They slid out their swords, ready to start slitting sleeping throats. The enemy moved forward.

Then, all at once, the silence was broken by screeching, cackling, blood-chilling screams.

The geese had woken and raged
against the strangers. Geese are
better at guarding than dogs.

Marcus Manlius woke. He
snatched his sword and gathered
his guards.

The Gauls panicked. Some
staggered backwards over the
cliff and fell screaming on to
the Tarpeian Rocks below.

The rest were driven back and killed. Cries of men mingled with the gabbling of the geese until the last attacker died and calm returned.

Torches were lit and the priests and the soldiers gathered near the temple of Juno.

"We were saved by the geese," Marcus Manlius said.

"A sign from the gods – a miracle," Marius said.

And Fabia's eyes glittered in the torchlight. "You can't kill them now," she said, and looked at me with fierce glee.

"We can't kill them now," Marius agreed.

Fabia smiled at me. "*Vae victis*," she said quietly. "*Vae victis* ... woe to the defeated."

I knew I had been defeated by the gods. And I deserved it.

AFTERWORD

The characters of Fabia and Brutus are not real. But much of the rest of the story is true ... probably.

The Gauls *did* invade Rome and the Roman army ran away. When the Gauls entered Rome the old senators met them in silence and were slaughtered. Marcus Manlius and his troop held the Capitol Hill and the temples for weeks, slowly starving, until Furius arrived.

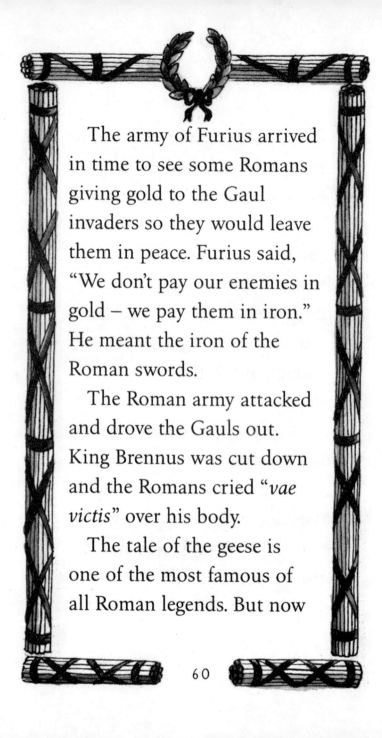

The army of Furius arrived in time to see some Romans giving gold to the Gaul invaders so they would leave them in peace. Furius said, "We don't pay our enemies in gold – we pay them in iron." He meant the iron of the Roman swords.

The Roman army attacked and drove the Gauls out. King Brennus was cut down and the Romans cried "*vae victis*" over his body.

The tale of the geese is one of the most famous of all Roman legends. But now

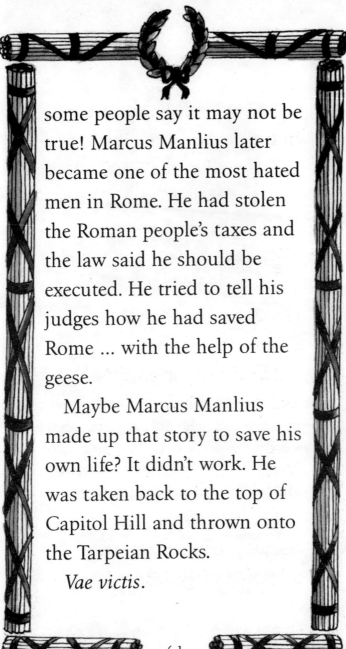

some people say it may not be true! Marcus Manlius later became one of the most hated men in Rome. He had stolen the Roman people's taxes and the law said he should be executed. He tried to tell his judges how he had saved Rome ... with the help of the geese.

Maybe Marcus Manlius made up that story to save his own life? It didn't work. He was taken back to the top of Capitol Hill and thrown onto the Tarpeian Rocks.

Vae victis.

ROME, AD 51

Deri is in prison. The outspoken Celt was
heard criticising Rome and now faces execution
in the morning. Luckily, his cell mate Caratacus is
a very special prisoner indeed - a British chief.
He believes there is a way to save both their
skins, but first he will need Deri's help.

Roman Tales are exciting, funny stories based
on historical events - short chapters and
illustrations throughout are perfect for
building reading confidence.

ISBN 978 0 7136 8960 0   £4.99

ROME, AD 64

Rome is a dangerous place. Especially on the day of the chariot races, and for a young girl. When Mary finds herself the only witness to a terrible crime, soon it is not just the thieves and drunks that she has to worry about, but someone far more cruel and powerful...

Roman Tales are exciting, funny stories based on historical events - short chapters and illustrations throughout are perfect for building reading confidence.

ISBN 978 0 7136 8970 9   £4.99

ROME, AD 113

Pertinax is helping prepare magnificent
dishes for a feast to be held by the great
lawyer Pliny. While the boy is working,
Pliny tells him the story of a terrifying ghost
who haunted a garden not unlike Pliny's own.
But there's no truth in ghost stories ... is there?

Roman Tales are exciting, funny stories based
on historical events - short chapters and
illustrations throughout are perfect for
building reading confidence.

ISBN 978 0 7136 8961 7   £4.99